Friends
Together

1 3 5 7 9 10 8 6 4 2

Copyright © Rob Lewis 2000

Rob Lewis has asserted his right under the Copyright, Designs and Patents
Act, 1988, to be identified as the author and illustrator of this work

First published in the United Kingdom 2000
by The Bodley Head Children's Books
Random House, 20 Vauxhall Bridge Road, London SW1V 2SA

Random House Australia (Pty) Limited
20 Alfred Street, Milsons Point, Sydney
New South Wales 2061, Australia

Random House New Zealand Limited
18 Poland Road, Glenfield
Auckland 10, New Zealand

Random House South Africa (Pty) Limited
Endulini, 5a Jubilee Road,
Parktown 2193, South Africa

The Random House Group Limited Reg. No. 954009
www.randomhouse.co.uk

A CIP catalogue record for this book is available from the British Library

ISBN 0 37032512 5

Printed in Singapore

Friends Together

Rob Lewis

THE BODLEY HEAD
LONDON

Clive and Ambrose had made a boat, and they were sailing on the lake with their friends.
"Look, there's a fish!" said Zoe.
"Stop leaping about," said Charles. "You will sink the boat."

SPLASH!
Zoe fell in the water.

And so did all her friends.

"Race you to the island," shouted Ambrose.

"What shall we do now?"
said Bernie.
"First we must make some plans,"
said Charles.
"No," said Charlotte. "Let's make
a fire first."

"Let's swim back to the shore," said Ambrose.
"No," said Clive, with his tummy rumbling, "let's find some food."
"No," said Zoe. "Let's make a flag and signal for help."
"No way," Maisie shouted, "let's just shout for help."

Bernie couldn't think of anything.
"What can I do?" he said.
But no one was listening. They had
all gone off to try their own ideas.

Charlotte found a big stick for a fire, but it was too heavy.

Ambrose tried to swim to the shore, but it was too far.

Clive looked for food, and then ate it all himself.

Maisie called for help,
but only Clive heard her.

Zoe jumped up and down,
but she didn't have a flag.

Charles drew plans in the sand, but crawly
creatures kept walking all over them.

At last Bernie had his idea.
"I know what we should do!" he shouted.
His friends came running.
"We should all work TOGETHER!"
he said.

So Charles made some more plans, and they all looked at them together.
"This is how you make a fire," he said. "And this is how you
wave for help!"

Together they collected wood for a fire.

Together they made a signal.
They used Charlotte's knickers as a flag.

Together they looked for food.
This time Clive saved it for later.

Together they sat by the fire and ate dandelion stew.

And together they sang songs under the stars.

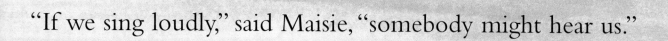

"If we sing loudly," said Maisie, "somebody might hear us."

Suddenly they saw a light on the lake.

It was the parents in a big boat.

"We saw your flag and we heard your singing," the parents said.
"Don't worry," said Bernie. "We are all safe."

"Because we all worked TOGETHER," said the friends, together.